For my wife Emily, my Mum,
and all good witches.

LITTLE TIGER PRESS LTD,
an imprint of the Little Tiger Group
1 Coda Studios, 189 Munster Road, London SW6 6AW
www.littletiger.co.uk

First published in Great Britain 2014
This edition published 2018
Text and illustrations copyright © Ian Cunliffe 2014
Ian Cunliffe has asserted his right to be identified as the author
and illustrator of this work under the Copyright, Designs
and Patents Act, 1988

A CIP catalogue record for this book is available
from the British Library

Printed in China
LTP/1800/2326/0718
2 4 6 8 10 9 7 5 3 1

This Little Tiger book belongs to:

_____

_____

_____

I Want to be a Witch

by
Ian Cunliffe

LITTLE TIGER
LONDON

When I grow up...

...I want to be a **witch**.
I'd like a **sparkly** hat,
covered in stars.

But I don't want **yucky** green hair like straw...

...And I wouldn't want to wear those **ugly**, curled-up boots.

I DON'T like bats, spiders or creepy-crawly things.

They give me the shivers!

But I REALLY DO love cats!

Bread for me,
fish for Cat.

Me and my cat do...

...EVERYTHING
together.

Bat-Cat & Pumpkin Girl!

Me and Cat
in Venice.

I definitely don't want any of these:
A bent, warty nose,
A big, hairy chin,

A crooked, squinty eye...

...Or gnarled, knobbly knees!

And I would **always** look after **MY** teeth.

I wouldn't mix any **horrid** potions
in a **smelly** old cauldron.

But a crystal ball and a magic wand *would* be very useful.

Hocus Pocus Poo,
A wizard I'll make you.
No longer just a cat,
In a pointy hat,
You can do
Spells too!

I wouldn't want to make friends with other, SCARY witches...

It never ends well.

I probably wouldn't turn
my brother into a frog...

But flying around on a broomstick would be...

Whoosh!

...REALLY fun!

When I grow up I want to be a
LOVELY witch...

...Just like my mum.